LITTLE
OWL
RESCUE

Rachel Delahaye

LITTLE TIGER

LONDON

Dedicated to the brilliant planet-friendly 18th Bath Brownies and to Tiya Constantine who loves trees
– Rachel

LITTLE

OWL

RESCUE

STRIPES PUBLISHING LIMITED
An imprint of the Little Tiger Group
1 Coda Studios, 189 Munster Road, London SW6 6AW

A paperback original
First published in Great Britain in 2020

ISBN: 978-1-78895-185-2

The Forest Stewardship Council® (FSC®) is a global, not-for-profit
organization dedicated to the promotion of responsible forest management
worldwide. FSC defines standards based on agreed principles for responsible
forest stewardship that are supported by environmental, social, and economic
stakeholders. To learn more, visit www.fsc.org

2 4 6 8 10 9 7 5 3 1

CONTENTS

The Sky Chairs

"Isn't this exciting?" Fliss shouted over the whirs and whoops. "I love the fair."

"Me too," Gabriel said, handing her his raspberry slushie to taste. Fliss slurped it and stuck her tongue out. It was stained a bright blue. Gabriel laughed. "You haven't changed a bit, Fliss!"

Gabriel was Fliss's oldest friend – they'd known each other since they were toddlers. He and his family had moved to France three years ago but they were back for a few days to visit friends. As a treat, Fliss and Gabriel had been allowed to go to the Big Fun Funfair – at night-time! Going at night was extra special because against the darkening sky, the fair looked magical with all its flashing lights, like a giant spaceship.

Fliss was full of fizzy drink and candyfloss and was happy just to walk around, watching the rides and the faces of the people on them. But Gabriel had other ideas.

"I spy the sky chairs!" he said. "Let's go!"

"I'm not sure," Fliss said. "I think I've eaten too much to go spinning round."

"Come on, it looks so much fun!"
urged Gabriel. "I've got a packet of
rainbow glow sticks. We can wave them
in the air. It'll be *très cool*!"

He gave her a handful of the clear
tubes that would glow neon as soon as
they were snapped. Fliss agreed that
waving rainbow wands high up in the

3

air would indeed be very cool – or *très cool*, like Gabriel said. She loved the way French words crept into his English language sometimes.

"All right then. But I warn you, I might throw up!"

"Only babies throw up. Let's go!" laughed Gabriel.

Fliss didn't usually like heights but after her recent adventures, helping baby animals in the wild, Fliss thought the sky chairs would probably be easy-peasy. And if it made Gabriel happy then she would be brave. She was surprised by how adventurous and confident he had become. When they were little he had been shy and scared of lots of things in the playground, even the slide! While the other kids played

on the monkey bars, he was happy
to play Fliss's games of Vet Hospital
instead, even though Fliss always
insisted on being the vet. Gabriel might
have changed but she hadn't – she still
wanted to be a vet!

Fliss and Gabriel sat in a seat that
dangled from chains attached to a
carousel. It was just like a normal swing,
apart from the safety bar that the ride
operator lowered on to their laps to stop
them from falling out. When the seats
were full, the music started and the
carousel began to turn. It made Fliss's
heart flutter. They were so high and
away from the lights of the fair below, it
suddenly seemed scarily dark...

"Here we go!" Gabriel said, kicking
his feet excitedly, rocking the swing.

The seats began to spin faster and faster and then flew out sideways, away from the central pillar that was rising into the air, lifting the swings higher. Fliss gasped as the ground dropped away beneath them and she gripped on to the safety bar.

"No need to do that," Gabriel said, grinning from ear to ear. "Do this!"

Fliss gasped again as Gabriel stretched out his arms as if he were a bird swooping through the sky.

"Are you a *poule mouillée*?" Gabriel asked.

"A what?"

"A *poule mouillée* – it means wet chicken. A scaredy-cat!"

"I am definitely not a wet chicken!" Fliss said. To show him, she let go of the bar and stretched out her arms even wider than he did.

"Now you're a flying wet chicken," Gabriel laughed.

Fliss felt more like an eagle than a chicken! She ignored her friend's teasing and enjoyed the moment. Below her dangling feet, lights twinkled like glitter and the people wandering through the fair looked as small as ants.

Straight ahead, Fliss could see streetlamps marking out the criss-crossing roads of the town and beyond that farms and fields, all grey-green in the dusky light. It looked like a living map.

Wouldn't it be incredible to see the world from this high every day? Fliss thought.

Then, out of nowhere, gusts of wind brought huge grey clouds towards them. The damp fog wrapped round everything like thick candyfloss and soon Fliss could no longer see her living map or even her hands in front of her face. Or Gabriel next to her.

"Gabriel?"

Fliss wanted him to call her a wet chicken and tell her that everything was OK, but there was no answer.

"Don't panic, Felicity," she said to herself sternly, using her full name just as her mum would. "It's only a cloud. It will pass in a minute. The ride will end soon."

But the cloud didn't pass and the spinning didn't slow down. In fact, it sped up. Fliss was whisked round and round. She reached out for Gabriel but he had disappeared… Oh no!

She tried to call for help but the wind whipped the words from her mouth. She squeezed her eyes shut and hoped the ride would stop.

Then suddenly it did.

Fliss was standing still, with solid ground beneath her feet. She waited for the dizziness to disappear and carefully opened her eyes. The cloud had cleared, revealing a beautiful royal-blue sky underlined by an orange glow, where the sun had just dipped below the horizon.

But the sun set ages ago, Fliss puzzled. *And where's the funfair, the noise, the people?*

They were all gone and Fliss got the feeling she was a long, long way from home.

The Night Glider

Fliss looked around. She was standing on a raised dusty road, which sloped on each side into crop fields below. Apart from the occasional clump of trees she couldn't see anything else – just miles and miles of farmland – and there was nothing to tell her where she was. Fliss knew from experience that she could be anywhere on Earth.

She had been transported before, finding herself in new countries and environments, and each time it meant one thing: a young animal needed her help.

Where she had been brought to this time, she had no idea, and apart from the flies that buzzed around her, there were no animals to be seen.

"I know you're there somewhere," Fliss said out loud. "Don't worry, I'll find you!"

It was easy to say but Fliss didn't know where to start looking. She turned in circles, wondering which way to walk. In every direction she saw the same thing: yellowing crops in neat rows, separated by little pathways, all rose-tinted by the beautiful apricot sunset. But then, over there, two fields up... What was that?

Something large and square was
sparkling in the last of the sun's rays. It
didn't look like an animal but it could
be a hut or a signpost. There was only
one way to find out.

Fliss ran down the dusty track and
along two fields, then turned into the
field where she'd seen the object. But as
soon as she ran down the slope towards

13

it, she lost sight of everything. The crops now towered over her head. The plants had long stalks, with peeling leaves and solid pods. They looked familiar but Fliss's mind was focused on locating the shiny object she'd seen. Now that her view was blocked, she had to hope that her sense of direction was good. She ran down a pathway between the rows, occasionally battling through clumps of the plants to get to the next path across, closer to where she wanted to be.

She was tired and about to give up when suddenly she saw it. Parked in the middle of the field was a huge white tractor. Her heart sank a little when she saw there was no one inside. No one who could tell her where she was and what animals could be found in the area.

But there was writing on the side in swirly red letters.

"King O' Corn, Aliceville, Texas, U.S.A.," Fliss nodded her head. "U.S.A. … I'm in America! America! And that must be sweetcorn!"

Fresh corn on the cob was one of the yummiest things ever. Her mother always gave them to her cooked but sometimes Fliss ate them raw. She loved how the sweet kernels popped in her mouth… Something in the distance caught her eye. A small white bird with huge wings was flying towards her. Even in the dying light it looked dazzling as it glided silently through the warm air. An owl. Definitely an owl. And as it came closer, Fliss recognized the telltale heart-shaped face.

"A barn owl," Fliss whispered as it flew over her head. "A beautiful barn owl."

She watched the owl swoop nearer. It was barely flapping its wings and yet it travelled quickly and smoothly. A bird of prey expert called Mr Howell had once visited Fliss's school. He had brought falcons, hawks and owls of all sizes that had been trained to come when he called. They had been incredible – so alert, with their staring eyes and their heads turning at the slightest sound. Fliss had been transfixed by the barn owl. The sleek feathers on his underside had been brilliant-white, and they had fanned out in a heart shape as perfect as a cookie-cutter on his face.

The owl
was gliding
low over the
field, right
above her. It
had a little field
mouse in its claws, and as it continued
overhead Fliss could see its jet-black
marble eyes and flat pointy beak.

That's strange, Fliss thought. *Why would
it come so close to me? It's not like I'm small
enough to eat and it has prey already – a
little mouse. Why didn't the owl gobble down
the mouse?*

"You've got chicks that need feeding!"
Fliss exclaimed to the sky. "That's why
you didn't eat the mouse. Maybe your
chicks need my help... Well, that's fine
by me. If I get to see loads of barn owls,

I think I'm going to enjoy being here in Aliceville, Texas!"

Fliss wasn't sure if she was right but the beautiful barn owl was the only animal she'd seen since she'd arrived. It was definitely worth investigating. Follow that owl! She ran as fast as she could along the path and back towards the dusty road, where she would be higher up and have a better view.

As she ran, she broke out in a sweat. The air was thick with heat and dust, the ground beneath her was dry and cracked. It was still warm now – the day must have been scorching hot. That beautiful yellow sunset was probably a relief for the animals and the farmers – the air would be turning cooler, just for a while.

I'd be nocturnal too if I lived in such a hot place! Fliss thought.

And as she stepped back up on to the track, she saw it. The white owl. It looked like nothing more than a scrap of paper on the breeze as it flapped towards a cluster of trees in the distance. Fliss watched as it circled a while, almost as if it was waiting for her, before disappearing into the woods.

King O'Corn

Fliss ran down the track and into the next cornfield along, disappearing once again between the rows of towering sweetcorn. After the endless scratch and dust of the dry corn leaves, Fliss was looking forward to being in the greener, shadier woods and couldn't wait to explore. She was sure the owl was leading her there for a reason.

But as soon as she broke through the corn thicket next to the woods,

she came upon a strange sight. There
was bright orange sawdust all over
the woodland floor and tree stumps –
maybe a hundred of them – that looked
as though they had been freshly cut.
Though the light was dim she could see
that further into the woods, where the
trees became thicker, there were more
stumps and newly fallen trees lying on
the ground. Then she saw the sign.

King O' Corn Farm
Clearing in progress for expansion
of crop fields. For more information
contact Herman.

They were chopping down the woods
to grow more corn!
Surely no animals would still be living

here with the noise of the chainsaws and the tree cutters coming and going with their trucks? Perhaps the owl hadn't entered the woods at all but had flown right through them and out the other side.

Just then, Fliss heard a hoot. It came from somewhere in the trees.

"Or maybe you're hanging on to your home until the end," she said anxiously. "Don't worry, I'm coming."

Tripping on scattered branches and logs in the hazy light, Fliss crept into the woods. She looked all around for signs of the barn owl or any other creatures that might be in trouble. Then she spotted it, right ahead. The white bird, much smaller now, with its wings tucked back in place, was pacing the ground by a tree stump, the mouse dangling in its beak.

Perhaps her nest was in the tree that was chopped down! Fliss thought. *That's why she's looking confused.*

Fliss began to panic. She was certain that the owl was a mother, and the mouse was a meal for her chicks. So where were her chicks now? Fliss wanted to run to the mother owl and comfort it but she stopped herself.

"Animals don't always feel like we do, and all vets know you should watch an animal first before doing anything."

Watching an animal to see how it behaved was the best way to find out the bigger picture. Maybe this owl didn't need her help after all. Then it would be terrible to scare her away!

Fliss ducked behind a tree stump
and watched, blinking in the fading
light, not wanting to miss a thing.
For a while nothing happened – the
owl just paced, but suddenly three
smaller owls staggered into the open
from behind a fallen tree. The nest
must have crashed to the ground!
Their bright white feathers were a little
ruffled but they didn't seem to be hurt.

Perhaps the surrounding trees had slowed their fall. Everything was fine!

Thank goodness I didn't act too quickly, Fliss thought. *And what a treat to be able to see a mother with her chicks.*

This owl family was fine, which meant Fliss would have to look elsewhere for the animal that needed her help. Right now, though, she would stay and watch what this pretty owl family did next.

The owl mother shared the mouse between the chicks. They squabbled over it – hopping about, flapping their wings and making such a fuss that Fliss could hardly see what was going on! All she knew was that they gobbled down the mouse in seconds. They must have been starving. Fliss wondered how long it had been since they last ate. She

remembered Mr Howell telling them
that mother barn owls weren't very good
parents – they often disappeared for
days, and sometimes slept in another
nest, away from their chicks. Maybe
she hadn't fed them in a while. *Or
maybe,* Fliss thought, looking at the tree
stumps, *all the farming has made it harder
to find food.*

Suddenly, without warning, the
mother launched herself off into the
woods. Her flight was totally silent and
Fliss wouldn't have noticed her leave if
she hadn't turned at the right moment.
Although it might be normal behaviour
for a mother owl, Fliss was worried.
Chicks on the ground could be food for
snakes or other creatures…

Phew! The mother had returned.

But she didn't land. She circled over the chicks below.

There was a frantic beating of wings and then one, two of the chicks made it off the ground and into the air, where they flapped like crazy. They were up for a few seconds before they landed awkwardly and off balance, like planes on a windy day. Then the mother flew off again and the two chicks tried once more, stretching out their wings this time, looking more confident and flying – actually flying! Without any hesitation they followed after their mother, which left just one.

The chick on the ground hopped into the air, testing its wings each time its feet were off the ground. But it wasn't getting the hang of it. Fliss looked in

the direction of the owls' flight but
there was no flash of white in the dark
tree canopy. They weren't circling back.
They had gone.

"The mother will return," Fliss said to herself. "She's probably just gone to find a new nest."

As the chick kept trying to fly, and each time landing with a graceless tumble on the ground, Fliss wanted more than anything to pick it up and give it a cuddle. But she knew the chick would learn to fly eventually and she shouldn't get in the way. Not unless something terrible was about to happen.

Horn and Claws

Fliss didn't know how long she had
waited for the mother to return, but it
was now night-time and some parts of
the woods were in total darkness. She
wouldn't have been able to see anything
at all if it weren't for the moonbeams
that made their way through the gaps
in the trees. A shaft of moonlight
shone through a section where the tree
chopping had created a big hole in the
canopy and it cast a light on the owl

chick. The poor thing had grown tired of trying to fly and now stood perfectly still, like a large white pebble.

What should I do? What should I do? Fliss's mind turned over and over, wondering if she should pick up the bird. It was now clear that the chick had been abandoned. She wouldn't be doing it any harm.

The first thing she had to do was introduce herself. If she just ran over and picked up the chick, it could damage a wing trying to get away or even die of fright. She had to be gentle but confident, because she knew that animals sensed if you were nervous and that could make them nervous too.

Fliss straightened up from her crouched position behind the tree stump

so she could be seen. But still the chick
didn't move. Perhaps it was too scared
to look round.

"Hey, little one," Fliss said softly. "I'm
not going to hurt you."

She began to walk forwards slowly,
placing each foot down very carefully so
she wouldn't trip on the uneven ground.
The chick was startled by the movement
and tried to fly away. It managed to
get up on to the tree stump, and then it
froze. Something had caught its eye.

Fliss looked up. There, shooting
through a shaft of moonlight, she saw a
bird. An owl!

"Is that your mother? So she did come
back for you!"

Fliss immediately started to move
away, not wanting to alarm the mother.

If she thought it was too dangerous to land, she might fly off again and never return. Although Fliss knew that barn owl parents weren't very protective, maybe this owl was different.

But as the owl flew through another patch of light, Fliss noticed that it wasn't beige and white, it was varying shades of brown. It wasn't a barn owl.

As the bird swooped closer, Fliss saw it had strange tufty feathers on its head. They looked almost like pointy cat ears or horns. A large tail fanned out behind it. Its eyes were yellow and piercing.

"A great horned owl!" Fliss gasped.

They were easy to identify because of their remarkable 'horns'. And they were so vicious, Mr Howell had explained in a funny voice, that they would eat anything they could get their claws into. Even other birds.

Fliss saw the intensity on its face as it drew near. Then its stumpy legs came down – huge four-toed talons splayed out on each foot. It was then that Fliss realized the horned owl was not planning to land.

It was after the chick!

If there was a time to get involved, it was definitely now. Shouting loudly to disturb the horned owl's concentration, Fliss ran forwards and grabbed the baby barn owl. She held it tightly against her chest and turned her back just in time. The attacker's strong wings whipped across her. Fliss braced herself for the scratch of razor-sharp talons or the dagger of a beak, but it never came. Realizing that its prey had been stolen, it was already flying away.

"That was so close," Fliss said aloud. She was panting, her heart beating fast with the adrenalin. "Thank goodness I was here or you might have been…"

She trailed off, not wanting to think what might have happened to the chick, and then she realized something. "Aha!"

she said, smiling.
"It's you. *You're*
the reason I'm
here, aren't
you?"

The chick
circled its head
as if it was trying
to understand.

"I just *knew* I was
going to enjoy being in
Texas," Fliss laughed. "But as much as
I'd like to spend time getting to know
you, I have to get you somewhere safe
before any other scary-faced owls come
looking for a bite to eat."

Fliss took the cardigan she'd tied
round her waist and wrapped the chick
in it. "I'm not sure where to start but

one thing's for sure – I can't leave
you here alone. We'll have to do this
together."

Fliss stared into the woods, wondering
what to do. There weren't any gliding
barn owls to show her the way. There
was no movement at all, apart from
down on the woodland floor where
the odd leaf rustled as tiny mammals
scuttled about. She saw something move
across the ground in front of them, lit
up by the moon. It darted as quickly as
it could into the undergrowth.

"Yes, run!" Fliss said. "Or you'll be
someone's dinner."

She frowned. With more and more
trees disappearing every day, soon there
would be nowhere for these creatures
to hide. And perhaps nowhere for the

owls to live either. With a big sigh, Fliss looked down into the heart-shaped face of the barn owl chick.

"Before we worry about the future, we need to think what to do right now."

Will You Be My Friend?

The woods were so dark that Fliss realized she'd never be able to find the barn owl's nest. She could hardly see a metre ahead, let alone a hole in a tree trunk.

"This rescue mission isn't going to be completed tonight, that's for sure!" she said. "We'll have to wait until dawn. But in the meantime, let's take a look at you."

Fliss wanted to check that the little owl hadn't been damaged in her rush

to save it. She'd tried to be gentle but
handling wildlife could be tricky – and
birds had such tiny bones, which could
easily break under too much pressure.
She just hoped that when she'd scooped
up the chick, she hadn't been too rough.
It had all happened so quickly.

There was more moonlight out in
the open so Fliss carried her precious
bundle back towards the cornfield. By
the edge of the crops, she crouched
down and unwrapped her cardigan,
revealing the little bird inside.

It was shivering a little. Maybe with
fear.

"Hello," Fliss said softly. "My name is
Fliss and I'm going to do everything I
can to help you. I want to be a vet when I
grow up so I've read plenty of books

about animals and watched lots of TV programmes too. I'd love to be your friend!"

She didn't know if it was possible to form a friendly bond with a bird, but she hoped her calm voice would soothe the little owl. It seemed to work. The chick looked up at her and twisted its head to one side as if to say hello.

"If we're going to spend some time together, I ought to give you a name. I can't just call you owl... Mmmm, let's see." Although Fliss loved all animals, she didn't know much about owls – just what Mr Howell had taught them, which didn't include working out whether they were boys or girls. Fliss decided it didn't really matter but she had a feeling the owl was a girl. She

looked down at the pretty little face with
its perfect cookie-cutter heart shape.

"That's it! You can be Cookie!"

Cookie hopped around and Fliss sat
back and watched for any awkward
movements or limping to show she
was injured. But the chick seemed fine.
More than fine! She jumped backwards
and forwards as if she were playing
hopscotch.

"There's nothing
wrong with you!"
Fliss said.

Cookie had
stopped
shivering and
seemed to
be enjoying
herself.

Fliss noticed that while the owl had mainly white plumage, the feathers on the tops of her wings and at the edges of her face were a light brown colour. She couldn't be very young, because in the video of nesting barn owls they had watched at school, the really young ones were strange-looking things – scrawny, white and fluffy, like startled balls of cotton wool!

Cookie was a lovely shape. Solid and smooth. If only Fliss could remember more of the information from Mr Howell's video... Oh yes! It said that by the age of eight or nine weeks they'd have tried flying, and from then on they got better and better at it but they still lived in their nest for months.

"So you're at least two months old,"

Fliss said, watching Cookie as she extended her wings and flapped a little. The chick ran back towards Fliss, wings still extended as if she was playing aeroplanes! The feathery tips brushed against Fliss's face.

"You may not be quite as advanced as your siblings but you're not far behind. You need to catch up quickly, though…" Fliss added, remembering something else Mr Howell had said. *If a barn owl chick can't get back into the nest, it's abandoned.* This had made Fliss sad at the time, and now she had a real-life abandoned chick in front of her, it was even more upsetting.

"That's what we're going to do," Fliss said with determination. "We're going to get you flying, so wherever your nest

is you can find it. Even if I can't. Let's
start now – there's no time to lose!"

Fliss didn't know how to teach an owl
to fly but she had to give it a go.

Cookie was hopping and flapping on
the small strip of land in front of them,
between the tree stumps at the edge
of the woods and the tall crops in the
cornfield. Fliss crouched and leaned
forwards to where the little owl had
stopped for a moment and was folding in
one of her wings.

Fliss tied her cardigan back round
her waist and wrapped her hands round
Cookie's soft body, lifting her off the
ground just a little. Then she shuffled
her hands so they were supporting
Cookie's feet and noticed immediately
how sharp those little talons were.

Ignoring the scratching sensation, Fliss looked into Cookie's dark eyes. They were like two little coals in the snow.

"I'm going to throw you in the air, OK? Then flap as hard as you can. Don't worry – if you fall, you're not far from the ground."

Fliss raised her hands up and down so that Cookie could get used to the movement. Just as she had hoped, the chick's reaction was to lift her wings to get her balance.

"Excellent, Cookie! Well done. Now for the real thing. Ready, steady … go!"

Fliss jerked her hands upwards and the little owl released her claws and let go. She flapped wildly in the air just in front of Fliss's face.

"Yes, Cookie! You're doing it!"

The chick was only in the air for a moment but she didn't fall down. Instead, she landed on Fliss's outstretched hand and quickly hopped up her wrist and along her arm. Before Fliss knew what was going on, Cookie had folded in her wings and was happily perched on Fliss's shoulder.

Fliss giggled. "Well that settles it. We're definitely friends now!"

To Catch a Mouse

The night air was fragrant with earthy smells and it was still warm, even though the sun had gone down a long time ago. Fliss breathed in deeply and smiled. *I'll never forget this moment*, she thought. Standing in a cornfield in Texas with a baby owl roosting on your shoulder didn't happen every day!

Fliss could feel the weight of Cookie and the light grip of her talons over her shoulder. Whenever Cookie shuffled, her

wing feathers brushed Fliss's cheeks and
Fliss had to try so hard not to laugh in
case she scared the little owl – but it was
Cookie that suddenly startled Fliss…

Psssh-cheee. Psssh-cheee.

What a strange noise. It sounded like
a snore and a jet of steam, and it was
really loud, right in Fliss's ear!

Psssh-cheee. Psssh-cheee.

Fliss decided that Cookie must be so
comfortable on her shoulder that she'd
fallen asleep. The snoring was cute but
now wasn't the time to be resting. Only
when Cookie had learned to fly could
either of them take a break.

"Come on, Cookie," Fliss coaxed.
"Back to work now. If we don't get you
in the air soon, you might never find
your family."

Fliss reached her hand across her body and carefully dislodged the owl, expecting it to wake up. Carefully, she pulled Cookie down and brought her other hand up to support the sleeping chick, cradling it in her arms.

Only Cookie wasn't asleep.

Psssh-cheee. Psssh-cheee.

Her little dark eyes were wide open, and with every odd screech she opened and closed her mouth. No, not a sleeping sound after all. Then what? Cookie let out a super loud rasp but kept her mouth wide open, making her look more like a brand-new baby than a fledgling.

"Aha! I know what you want," Fliss said. "Food! You didn't get any of the mouse, did you?"

Fliss remembered the owlets squabbling over the mouse that the mother had dropped. Perhaps it was because they weren't used to eating outside of the nest, or maybe the stronger chicks were just looking after themselves, but Cookie hadn't managed to get her beak anywhere close. Now she was hungry.

What do barn owls eat? Fliss asked herself. She thought hard, trying to recall Mr Howell's talk. *Ugh, why didn't I listen more carefully to the most important bit?* Usually she paid close attention, but this time she hadn't been able to stop staring at the majestic birds he'd brought with him! Knowing an animal's diet was key to providing it with good care and Fliss was cross with herself. But it wouldn't help to dwell on what she couldn't remember, she had to use her common sense.

Obviously owls ate mice – but what about insects or worms, which would be much easier to catch? Fliss couldn't be sure. Her best friend Ella had once tried

to feed cheese to a baby mouse she had
found on the pavement and it didn't end
well. It was never a good idea to guess. It
would have to be a mouse then, Fliss
decided. It was the only thing she was
certain of. She didn't know if she could
kill another creature, even if it was part
of nature's cycle, but she would worry
about that when the time came. First she
had to find a mouse!

"Your clever mother caught one in a
cornfield," Fliss said, placing Cookie
back on her shoulder. "So hold on tight,
because that's where we're going."

As Fliss stepped between the rows of
corn, the scraggy leaves brushed against
her and Cookie clung tighter, nuzzling
into Fliss's hair for protection. Here
the corn was fat and ready. Fliss could

see the cobs in the moonlight – bulging parcels clinging to the tall stems, each with a tuft of fibres sprouting from the top like hair. She would have loved to crunch into one of those sweet pods but she probably shouldn't steal from the farmer's crop and besides, it was unfair to eat while Cookie was so hungry. She had to help this young animal in need before she could think about herself.

Fliss continued walking deep into the field, her eyes on the rows of corn either side of her path. But there was no sign of a mouse or anything other than the winged insects and moths that flittered against her face. Fliss couldn't give up trying.

The rustling of the corn plants as she brushed by them sounded loud in the stillness of the night. It was only when Fliss stopped to wipe the sweat from her brow that she noticed the difference. When she wasn't moving it was so quiet. Of course! If there was any chance of catching a mouse, then marching noisily through the field was going to ruin it. Fliss remembered how the mother barn owl had swooped over the corn – she was perfectly silent.

"You should always learn from animals," Fliss muttered to herself, shaking her head. "How could I forget such an important lesson? Cookie, from now on we're going to have to be stealthy."

Fliss put her foot forwards, but immediately the plants swooshed and scratched. It was no good. They would have to be absolutely still. Perhaps Cookie would have a better chance on her own.

"I just make a lot of noise and scare everything away. Let's see how you do, shall we?" Fliss said, taking Cookie from her shoulder and placing her on the ground. They both stood quietly, listening for the teeniest of crunches and rustles among the corn.

Then Cookie heard something. Her head twisted sideways, locating the sound.

Go on, Cookie, Fliss willed. *Find your dinner!*

Cookie hopped off the pathway, into the crops and out of sight. Fliss didn't know what to do. If she didn't follow, she might lose Cookie. But if she did follow, she'd create too much noise…

Suddenly, there was a noise louder than any Fliss could make. It roared like a beast, with a crackle like a bonfire. If there had been any mice nearby, they'd have run away. Fliss started to think that perhaps she should too.

Because whatever it was, it sounded angry.

The Beast

"Cookie! Cookie!" Fliss cried urgently. "We have to go. Now!"

Growling, roaring, crackling. Was it a herd of angry bulls stampeding through the crops? Fliss had no idea what was making the noise, only that it was getting closer.

She desperately wanted to run.

"Cookie!" she called again but her voice was drowned out by the sound and there was no sign of the little owl. Cookie had hopped deep into the undergrowth.

Fliss couldn't leave without her. But she couldn't just stand there either.

To avoid danger I need to see what I'm dealing with, she thought.

Fliss jumped as high as she could, over and over again, trying to see above the tall corn plants. But no matter how hard she tried, she couldn't see anything except the tips of the corn in the moonlight and the dark sky above.

"Argh!" she shouted in frustration. There was only one thing left to do – head back to the dusty track and get a clearer view. But that meant leaving Cookie.

"If I can't see what's coming until it's too late, then Cookie won't have any chance at all," Fliss convinced herself.

She dropped her cardigan on the path so she could find her way back to the exact spot she had last seen Cookie and ran back towards the track. The roaring continued and Fliss found herself short of breath from running in the sticky warm air, and also from fear. She felt as if she were being hunted.

Don't be silly, Fliss. Whatever it is can't see you! she told herself.

It was easy to fear what you didn't

know, and if you were unsure,
sometimes it was better to slow down
and work out what it *wasn't*. And it
probably *wasn't* angry bulls because as
far as Fliss could tell, there were only
cornfields for miles, not cattle farms.
There had to be a simple explanation.

As Fliss ran up the slope to the dusty
track, she saw it.

In the distance, vast beams of light
swept over the field, making the
sweetcorn look like skinny dancing
ghosts. Behind them were giant
machines – a row of them with huge
rotating arms, each with blades sharp
enough to cut down anything in their
path. Combine harvesters. They were
harvesting the sweetcorn!

Cut down anything in their path…

"Oh no! Cookie!" Fliss yelled, speeding back down into the field.

She ran in a blind panic, tripping over the cardigan she'd left as a marker. Her knee hit the ground with a thwack and she cried out in pain. But there was no time to worry about her own injuries – if she didn't get to Cookie in time, she'd have failed in her mission to rescue and protect animals in need. And that would cause her far more pain than a scratched knee.

Fliss snatched up her cardigan and got to her feet, trying to hear any sound of Cookie hopping around in the corn, but the approaching harvesters were even noisier than before and it was impossible.

"Cookie!" she cried as loud as she could.

Stepping off the pathway and pushing her way through the corn, Fliss ignored the discomfort of the scratchy leaves and paper-dry stalks that nicked at the skin on her legs and face. She shouted for the little owl as the machines advanced, their long light beams now dancing on the corn around her. It wouldn't be long until the harvesters were right there, cutting up the corn, shredding the stalks and destroying everything at her feet.

Fliss pushed on, her nose full of the dust that billowed from the shredded crops in clouds. When the dust settled, it covered everything in a fine, itchy powder. But there was no time to wipe it away. With every second, the harvesters were getting closer and then – Cookie!

Just ahead of her, the chick was in half flight – flapping in the air before falling back down again.

"It's not the time for flying practice now!" Fliss shouted. "Cookie, come back!"

But whether Cookie was chasing a mouse or enjoying the feeling of being in the air, she clearly wasn't ready to stop. Fliss quickened her step in an effort to catch up with her feathered friend. She lost sight of the owl for a moment, and then suddenly Cookie was lit up – a luminous white bird in the harvesters' high-beam headlights.

They were here. Just metres away.
The machines growled deafeningly and
the crunch of the crops between their
blades sent a shiver of terror down
Fliss's spine.

"Cookie, please!" she shouted,
running towards the owl and right

up to the mouths of the harvesters
that were quickly eating up the space
between them.

Fliss lunged forwards to catch Cookie
but the owl flapped and caught the
air beneath her wings, sending her up
and over the next row of corn. Fliss
followed in terror, her breath caught
in her throat. The lights were now
dazzling, blinding her if she looked
at them straight on. She needed to
get out of there fast! But not without
Cookie. Fliss pushed through to the
next row of corn and there, in a cloud
of brilliantly lit dust particles, Cookie
hung above the corn, wings fully
extended. It was now or never.

Using all her strength, Fliss leaped up
and snatched Cookie from the air.

She fell to the ground with a thud.
Ouch! But it didn't matter. She had the
owl and now they needed to run. With
the growling, crunching noise following
just behind, Fliss sprinted as fast as
her tired legs would carry her. She ran
back towards the track, the harvesters
still so close that their beams lit the way
ahead of her. Fliss's ears were full of
the jarring sound. She turned to see how
far behind the
machines
were, and
that's
when she
tripped.

Glow in the Dark

Fliss yelled at them to stop but it was no good. In the cabins of the harvesters, the drivers were busy checking switches and dials. They weren't looking down and so they couldn't see the little girl clutching a tiny owl, lying in the gloom of the alley between the corn. Fliss squeezed her eyes tight … and everything went black.

She opened her eyes and blinked at the sudden darkness around her. The lights had gone. When her eyes

adjusted, she saw that the harvesters
had swung round and were heading
back the other way, rumbling across
the cut corn towards the farm.

Fliss lay flat on her back, her heart
pounding, overcome with relief. Then
she started to laugh. She laughed and
laughed and couldn't stop. Cookie
hopped on to her tummy and tried to
look into her face, curious about the
funny noise she was making. This only
made Fliss giggle more, and Cookie
dug her claws in to keep her balance
as Fliss's tummy jiggled with laughter.
That hurt enough to make her stop.

"When I realized I'd be rescuing a
little owl, I had no idea it would be
quite this dangerous!" Fliss said, sitting
up and taking Cookie in her arms. "You

must be the most troublesome owlet in the whole of Texas. Maybe even the whole of America!"

Fliss placed Cookie on the ground and stood up to brush herself down. She was covered in dust and flecks of corn, and probably bruises too, although it was too dark to see. *Thank goodness for the moon*, she thought, looking at the white bird at her feet. *Without it, I'd be lost.* Humans are definitely *not* nocturnal animals. She crouched down and held out her arm, as she'd seen Mr Howell do with his birds of prey.

"Up you hop, Cookie," she said. And the owl did. "Clever girl! Come on, let's get back to the woods so we're closer to your family. We'll have a short rest and think about what to do next."

Walking back to the tree stumps, Fliss
felt a gnawing ache in her stomach. Poor
Cookie hadn't eaten yet but how could
Fliss think clearly with her own tummy
churning? She popped Cookie down on
one of the stumps and stepped towards
the cornfield, where a few stalks had
escaped the harvesters. There on the
ground was a fallen pod. The farmer
surely wouldn't miss this one. She

peeled back the stringy husk to reveal the fresh sweetcorn, gleaming like beads in the moonlight.

"Oh, that is so good!" Fliss sighed, chomping on the refreshing corn. "I guess that's why they harvest at night, so the corn is cooler and better to store."

She turned to look at Cookie. The little owl was tilting her head as if she was trying to understand Fliss's language. A moonbeam revealed her standing patiently, twisting her heart-shaped face from side to side – clockwise then anticlockwise. But Fliss's eyes were quickly drawn to another, darker figure lurking on the ground just behind the stump. Although it was in the shadows, Fliss could see it skulking. It was the size of a large cat but cats didn't have long bushy tails like that… What was it?

The shape moved round the tree
stump, occasionally lifting itself on its
hind legs to look up. Sniffing perhaps.
Whatever it was, it was interested in
Cookie… It shuffled round and then, hit
by another beam of moonlight through
the trees, Fliss could see exactly what it
was. It was grey and white, with black
markings across its nose and eyes – a
raccoon!

Fliss had seen raccoons in documentaries
about animals in America. She'd always
thought they looked quite funny and
sweet, with their big whiskers, bandit-
mask markings and pointy noses – but
they were often described as pests. They
raided rubbish bins and destroyed
everything in their hunt for food. If they

got into your house, they could trash it in minutes. They were fierce scavengers and would eat anything. On one programme, a woman described how a raccoon attacked her small dog…

Uh-oh. *That's why it was interested in Cookie!*

Without stopping to think what might happen, Fliss ran at the raccoon. "Shoo! Get away!"

But the raccoon didn't move.

"I said get out of here!" Fliss shouted. She ran right up to it, ready to nudge it away with her foot if needed. But there was something strange about the furry hunter. It wasn't scared of her, even though she was much bigger. Why wasn't it running away?

The raccoon waited until Fliss was

standing right in front of it before
it turned and lunged at her, making
a weird noise – something between a
growl and a hiss. Fliss saw its eyes like
green marbles. Its fangs too – sharp
white points. Quickly she ran backwards
and hoped it would follow her, away
from Cookie. But the raccoon wasn't
going to be put off.

It started leaping up at the tree stump.

"No!" she yelled. But it didn't make a difference.

Quick, Fliss, think of something, she thought to herself. *How can I scare it away?*

Remembering that earlier she had been scared by noises she didn't understand, Fliss suddenly had a brilliant idea. She pulled a thin plastic tube out of her pocket.

"We're frightened of what we don't know," she said softly. "So what do you think of this?"

She snapped the tube in three places, which quickly set off a chemical reaction inside it. The glow stick turned red, orange, yellow, green, blue – all the colours of the rainbow – and Fliss boldly stepped forwards, waving it at

the raccoon
and making
the weirdest
noises she
could think
of.

"Bet you
haven't seen
one of these
before," she sang.

The raccoon wasn't so quick to
fight back this time. Instead it seemed
mesmerized by the wand and then,
without warning, it scuttled off.

Fliss ran towards the little owl and
crouched down. "Oh, Cookie, the
world is a dangerous place when you
don't have a home," she said, suddenly
thinking of her own home, so far away.

Cookie leaped on to her shoulder, nestling once again in her hair.

"Don't worry. I'm not going anywhere. Not until I know you're one hundred per cent safe."

Lessons from an Owl

Fliss sat down on the stump, looking out at the moonlit field, now empty of corn. She felt just as empty of ideas.

Cookie couldn't fly yet – not properly anyway. Although she tried, she kept coming down after a few seconds like a kite with no wind. Fliss had to get Cookie back to her nest as soon as possible, in case another sneaky raccoon or a horned owl came by.

"But how can I help you?" Fliss said,

reaching up to stroke the owl's tummy feathers. "I can't fly either, so I'll never be able to find your family or a new nest safely up in the trees."

Fliss reached across, took Cookie from her shoulder and placed the owl on her lap. They sat in silence, listening to the gentle swoosh of the light night breeze in the treetops and the occasional scuttle among the debris of the corn in the field.

Psssh-cheee. Psssh-cheee.

Fliss was woken from her worries by that familiar noise. Cookie was hungry.

Psssh-cheee. Psssh-cheee.

"OK we can look for food again. But if you want a mouse, you're going to have to hunt for it yourself," Fliss said. "One crunch of my feet on that dry grass and they'll run away. But you can't go far. I'm keeping you in my sights this time."

She popped Cookie on the floor.
The owl listened intently, twisting her
head this way and that, hearing noises
that Fliss couldn't. Every rustle, every
shuffle – Cookie was listening. Fliss
marvelled at how she could move her
head right round and side to side in
order to hear the noises more clearly.
Her big circular face was like a satellite
dish, rotating to get the best signal.

But if Cookie did hear a mouse, she wasn't going to chase after it. After only a few seconds the owl bounced back towards Fliss and fluttered clumsily up to her perch on Fliss's shoulder.

"I'm not surprised you're scared," Fliss soothed. "I would be too, after everything that's happened."

Fliss sat still and allowed herself to think of home. How would she ever get back? She knew from previous adventures that she could only return once the baby animal was safe. But sitting here in the dark, straining to see anything in the gloom, she had no idea how to make Cookie safe. She felt bruised and sore, tired and helpless.

"Come on, Fliss, think!" she said to herself, crossly. "What would a vet do?"

Fliss thought back to the research she had done into being a vet. One of the first things she'd learned was that you had to respect the animal.

"Well, I definitely respect animals," she said. "More than anything! I could do all the research in the world, but animals will always know their environment better then me…"

Fliss jumped up excitedly. "That's it! *You're* the teacher!"

Cookie made a funny noise – it sounded like a little laugh.

Fliss giggled. "Miss Cookie, all this time you've been teaching me how to be an owl. And finally I think I've worked out the most important lesson: listening."

Fliss had been nervous about going

back into the woods to find Cookie's
mother. It seemed so pointless when she
couldn't see anything. A few steps past
the stumps, the moonlit night faded into
total darkness. The thought of being in
the pitch-black and not being able to see
frightened her, but for animals it wasn't
such a big deal. Not if they used their
other senses. Fliss thought of Cookie's
stillness when listening and how she tried
to locate the sound by turning her head...

With Cookie tucked into her neck,
Fliss would be able to feel if the
owl was alerted by a noise from its
movements against her cheek and hair.
And if Cookie didn't hear her mother
or her hungry brothers and sisters up
in their nest, then perhaps her mother
would hear Cookie and her funny

sounds. Right on time, Cookie spoke.
Psssh-cheee. Psssh-cheee.

Fliss walked past the tree stumps and deep into the wooded areas that hadn't yet been hacked down by King O' Corn. The trees were denser here and hardly any moonlight made it through the foliage.

She felt nervous and lost but Fliss had made her mind up – she wasn't walking out again until she'd found the barn owls' nest.

Treetop Thrills

Looking up, Fliss could just about see the moonlight on the leaves at the very tops of the trees, but at ground level it was so dark she might as well have been wearing a blindfold.

She held out her arms in front of her, feeling for trees in the way, and placed her feet cautiously on the ground. Although she couldn't see, she noticed so much more, like the slightest puff of breeze on her face and twigs snapping underfoot. Rustles in the bushes made the hairs on her arms stand on end, but she knew it was probably nothing more than a squirrel or a mouse. Every now and then she stopped and held her breath, so that she and Cookie could listen carefully to their surroundings.

It seemed that there was nothing out there and Fliss wondered if she should think again – perhaps she could find a friendly farmer who might know a rescue centre for Cookie. But it was always better to keep a baby animal with its family if possible, and she was determined not to give up. She kept moving, slow as a sloth, reaching out for obstacles and stopping for sound checks. And then suddenly she felt Cookie's head brush against her cheek as it swivelled.

Fliss stopped. "I can't hear a thing, Cookie. Have you got an itch?"

But Cookie continued to rotate her head. She was trying to pinpoint the exact location of a noise. What noise? Fliss could only hear the slight rustle of the bird by her ear.

Then Cookie shrieked. The sound was loud but squeaky, like trainers on a smooth floor. *Scree-ee-ee.* Cookie had never made that sound before. From somewhere in the distance, a similar squeak came back – a high-pitched shrill. They were calling to each other.

"You clever girl, Cookie," Fliss said. "I'd never have heard that if it was just me."

Cookie called again, and again the call was returned.

"Got it," said Fliss. "We're walking straight ahead, towards the sound."

Stepping carefully so she didn't fall, Fliss made her way deeper into the woods. Every now and then Cookie and the other owl exchanged cries, and Fliss felt that they were getting closer. Closer to reuniting Cookie with her family.

High up in the canopy, caught in a smudge of faint moonlight, a huge white bird swooped down towards them, before vanishing into the darkness.

Fliss stood still, straining her eyes to see where it had gone and Cookie sat quietly on her shoulder.

Out of nowhere, Fliss felt a soft billow of air waft against her cheek, which she knew wasn't a Texas breeze. It was the bird.

"I think that's your mother," Fliss said, feeling a chill of excitement.

The mother called from high in the treetops just as her wings caught the moonlight once again. Was she returning to a nest? Fliss wasn't going to take her eyes off the owl for one second.

Yes! She could just make out the mother landing on a branch and a hole in the tree trunk. A new nest, perhaps. The beautiful owl hooted once again before ducking inside and Cookie returned the call – *scree-ee-ee*. It was definitely her mother! And even if the mother owl hadn't been the best parent in the animal kingdom, Fliss was determined to return her baby to her.

Fliss stood at the base of the tree where the mother had landed and realized it wasn't going to be easy. With Cookie still unable to fly, how was she going to get her into the nest? Fliss didn't like the idea of climbing all the way up there… But what else could she do? She ran her hands up and down the trunk, feeling for branches, but there were none.

93

"What would an animal do?" Fliss closed her eyes and pictured climbing animals, like monkeys and squirrels, imagining how they would solve such a problem. They would climb a nearby tree and swing across. Of course!

Fliss felt around for a neighbouring tree. She found it and reached up, managing to locate a branch. She could just about wrap her hands around it. The owl on her shoulder held tight as Fliss pulled herself up, and then felt for the next rung of the tree ladder. She found one, then another and another. Luckily this tree seemed fairly easy to climb – although doing it in the dark was going to be risky.

"Here we go, Cookie. If I slip, then we're both going to have to learn to fly. Fast!"

Cookie snuggled against her ear as if

she understood that Fliss was nervous.

"I'm only joking. I know I can do it. I've had to climb trees before, to rescue animals or stay out of danger. I'm quite good at climbing, really. The key is to never look down."

Looking down was a terrible idea if you were scared of heights, like Fliss, because it could make you dizzy. But there was nothing to see but darkness anyway, so Fliss concentrated on the light at the tops of the trees and kept moving. She pulled herself further up the tree, taking her time. The tree trunk narrowed the higher she went and Fliss found it easier to wrap her arms round it and hold herself securely. The branches got closer together too, so the problem wasn't finding the next one to move to, but avoiding knocking her head or snagging her clothes – things that might throw her off balance.

Eventually, she'd climbed so high she had reached moonlight. She was far above the ground and everything below her feet was wrapped in darkness. Her fear of heights melted away. At that moment all that mattered was the pretty owlet on her shoulder and her determination to get it home.

"So where is home?" she asked Cookie. "It has to be around here somewhere."

Scree-ee-ee. The sound was so loud, it vibrated in her ear. But it didn't come from Cookie.

It came from the owl next door.

Air Hop

Cookie shuffled impatiently, tickling Fliss's cheek.

"I know we're close, Cookie," Fliss said. "But please don't tickle me! I need to think."

Scree-ee-ee. Cookie screamed in her ear and stamped on her shoulder, making her giggle even more.

"I tell you what, if you're going to continue to be a wriggle-bottom, I'm going to need a safety harness."

Fliss carefully pulled her cardigan from her waist and looped it round her back, tying the arms together on the other side of the tree trunk. Instantly she felt more relaxed and a lot safer. She pulled aside a thin branch, revealing the next-door tree. There were white feathers at the mouth of a hole. It had to be the nest! But even though it was in sight, it wasn't in reach, and Fliss's plan to swing across like a monkey wasn't going to work.

"Oh, Cookie, it's no good," Fliss wailed. "What are we going to do?"

She sat down on the perfect seat of a forking branch and sighed heavily. How was she going to get Cookie into her nest? She wanted to cry but her vet's oath to help animals in danger stopped her. She had to go on, she *had* to!

There was nothing wrong with taking a rest though, so Fliss allowed herself to relax and thought of good things to lift her mood. Like nature and how incredible it was that the animal kingdom lived on so many levels – from tunnels in the ground, to the thinnest twigs on the tops of trees. It was amazing, and who ever would have thought that she would be up here in the trees, seeing the world like a bird.

Just then, Fliss noticed that the sky had lightened a little.

Unlike sunset with its rosy-golden tint, the dawn sun peeping over the horizon was as yellow as egg yolks, lighting the sky around it bright blue and picking out a few thin white clouds. Fliss realized that she had the best seat in the house for this spectacle. Around her, other birds were waking up with little cheeps and flutters and within hours the woods would be awake with daylight animals. But not owls.

Feeling more positive, Fliss stroked the owl on her shoulder. "Time to get you to bed, Cookie. Shall we try again?"

If she lay down on the branch and spread her weight evenly, it might just work. She untied her cardigan…

"Nearly there," Fliss said, edging along slowly, her stomach churning with nerves.

Halfway along the branch it started to bend and judder. Fliss considered whether it would be safer to stand and leap across like a squirrel but her human instincts held her back. Then the branch dipped suddenly and Fliss shuffled

back to the safety of the tree trunk and re-tied herself to the tree.

"It's no good, Cookie," she said. "I'll get you home. But we're going to have to climb back down and think of another way."

Cookie responded by hopping off her shoulder and all the way down her arm.

"Where are you going? No, Cookie!" Fliss shrieked as the owl leaped off her arm and on to the branch, moving further along to where it thinned out. "What are you doing?"

Holding back her panic, Fliss tried to coax Cookie towards her. If the owl were to fall there was nothing she could do...

"Cookie, come on, little one."

To her relief, the owl turned and hopped back. She jumped on to Fliss's hand and looked into her eyes. She tilted her heart-shaped face one way then the other.

"What are you saying?" Fliss said, sensing something strange in her little friend's behaviour.

Then Cookie made a rasping sound and blinked slowly before moving back along the branch. Fliss watched as the little owl spread her wings. She desperately wanted to crawl after Cookie and drag her to safety, but she knew that sometimes you have to trust nature.

Fliss held her breath. The moment seemed to last forever, and then… Flap! Cookie let go of the branch. She was flying!

Just a short air hop to the other tree but she did it, landing perfectly.

"Yes, Cookie!" Fliss whooped. "You amazing, wonderful little owl!"

Cookie was clearly pleased with herself because she flew right back again, settling on Fliss's shoulder where she nuzzled her. Fliss was certain that she could feel a cold little beak against her cheek, like a kiss.

"Don't get too cocky now!" she laughed. "Although I'm glad you came back for a cuddle. This time, you need to go and you need to stay."

Cookie spread her wings – white with light brown tips, as if she'd dipped them in tea. She twisted her head to look at Fliss one last time and then flew.

Fliss watched her go – just one beat

of those
splendid
wings
and she
was home.
Without
hesitation,
Cookie ducked into
the nest hole.

"I hope they left some food for you,"
Fliss said softly. "And I hope they
realize what a wonderful little owl you
are."

She wiped away a tear and looked out
over the woods. With her little feathered
friend safely back in her nest, surely it
was time for her to go home too?

The Final Flight

With fingers of daylight creeping
through the branches, Fliss could
now see how terrifyingly high she had
climbed. She had conquered situations
far harder than this, but she was
tired and a little heart-sore. Although
returning Cookie to safety had been
her goal, she was sad that their time
together was over.

"I'll just rest for a moment," she said
to herself.

Secured in her seat of branches, the cardigan tight around her like a harness, Fliss took a moment to enjoy the sunrise. It was a magnificent sight, but she wanted to experience it with her other senses first, just as she had learned to do at night. The warmth, the smells, the sounds of life awakening… She smiled and shut her eyes.

They had barely closed when her head felt as if it was spinning. Faster and faster. Was she falling? Had her cardigan come loose? Oh no!

Fliss's eyes flew open and her heart leaped to her throat. She was in darkness and she was spinning! She blinked, trying to work out what was happening. Then there was a loud moan next to her. *Gabriel?*

"I feel sick," Gabriel muttered, one

hand across his stomach, the other
clinging on to the safety bar.

Fliss tipped back her head and laughed.
She was back, still on the sky chairs,
flying as high as an eagle. Or an owl.

"It's not funny," groaned Gabriel.

Fliss felt a rush of happiness. "Come
on, stick your arms out like a bird. It
feels wonderful!"

As the sky chairs spun, Fliss looked out past the town at the farms in the distance. It was still night and the farm vehicles were heading home, their headlights dancing over the rocky farm tracks. She had a flashback of the combine harvesters and a sense of unease nagged at her happiness.

"Are you feeling sick?" Gabriel gulped.

"No," Fliss replied. "But I'll feel better when we're down on the ground."

"Me too," said Gabriel. "I hate this ride."

Fliss didn't hate the ride but she'd remembered the King O' Corn Farm sign about clearing the trees. She had to contact the farmer and local animal groups to let them know about the barn owls. She had to do something. If not, then Cookie, her family and all the woodland creatures would have nowhere to nest and hide.

The ride eventually ended and Gabriel headed for the toilets, staggering as if he were on a boat in a storm.

"I'll wait here," said Fliss, trying not to laugh.

Then someone called in a funny high voice. "Flissy, Flissy, Floo!" There was no mistaking who it was. Only her best friend Ella would shout out such a silly thing in front of lots of people. Ella ran at Fliss and wrapped her arms round her in a huge hug. "Is your French friend still here?" she asked.

"Yes, but he's not feeling very well. We just went on the sky chairs!"

"I love the sky chairs. Will you go on

them again with me? I'm here with my family, and my little brother is too small for anything but the teacups."

"Sorry, Ella. My parents are picking us up in a minute."

"Hang on, what's that? And *that*? And *that*!" Ella wrinkled her nose and plucked flakes of grass from Fliss's top, and a pure-white feather that was sticking out from behind her ear.

"Where have you been, Fliss?"

"On a Texas owl adventure!" Fliss replied, just as Ella's dad arrived with Ella's very tired-looking brother.

"Oh, hello there, Felicity! What have you been up to?"

"She's been on the Texas howl adventure, y'all!" Ella said, with a pretend American accent. "Is that some new ghost train ride or something?"

Fliss opened her mouth to correct her but decided it was probably better if she didn't have to explain. Besides, Ella had moved on and was now begging her dad for candyfloss. Eventually he gave in.

"Hooray! See you soon, Flissy Floss!"

"Bye, Ella," Fliss laughed, shaking her head.

Gabriel appeared soon after, still looking wobbly, and they went to meet Fliss's parents for a lift back home.

Over a late-night snack, Fliss and Gabriel's parents listened to their stories of the funfair – about the huge candyflosses and the ghost train and, of course, the sky chairs. Gabriel told everyone that it was *très amusant*. Fliss thought it was lots of fun too, and she decided not to mention that actually Gabriel had felt sick for most of the ride.

"I flew like an *oiseau*!" Gabriel exclaimed, making everyone laugh as he swooped around the kitchen like a bird. It reminded Fliss of something she needed to do.

She excused herself from the table and

went to the family computer, where she composed and sent an email to King O' Corn Farm, telling them about the woodland – how it was home to precious animals, including the magnificent barn owl. Then Fliss found the leaflets that Mr Howell had handed out at school. There was a contact email and she wrote to him of her worries about land clearing in Texas. Mr Howell must have been up late, tending to his owls, because he replied straight away saying he knew owl rescue centres all over America and would alert them right away. Satisfied that she'd done everything she could to help her owl friends, Fliss rejoined the fun at the table, her heart light as a feather.

Later, after they'd got ready for bed and Gabriel had talked and talked and then fallen fast asleep, Fliss found herself still wide awake. It had been such an exciting time – having Gabriel's family to stay, going to the funfair at night, the candyfloss and raspberry slushies, the sky chairs and then … finding herself in Aliceville, Texas.

Her heart skipped as she remembered the attack of the horned owl, the fright of the giant harvesters and the vicious raccoon. But her heart fluttered most of all when she remembered Cookie's curious little face and the bond she had made with the beautiful owl chick.

On the other side of the room, Gabriel's gentle snoring reminded her of Cookie's funny noises. Worried she would laugh out loud and wake him up, Fliss looked for a distraction.

Outside the bedroom window, the night was velvet-black and Fliss pushed her nose against the glass to look at the full moon that hung like a mobile among the twinkling stars. Something caught her eye. A piece of paper on the wind?

No, it was a white bird. By the light of the moon, it appeared luminous and Fliss held her breath as she watched it glide closer, silent and graceful. A barn owl.

"Don't go," she whispered.

But it didn't fly past, it looped
upwards then dipped, then up again

before swooping down. It was making
a shape! Was it... It couldn't be...
It was! It was a heart. Perfect, like a
cookie-cutter.

"Top marks for flying, Cookie!"
whispered Fliss. "You're an expert
now!"

The owl stretched her wings and
flew away, gliding like a feather on the
surface of a pond, off into the night.
This time Fliss was certain she'd gone.

But then a squeak echoed from
somewhere in the distant darkness.
Scree-ee-ee.

"Goodnight to you too, Cookie,"
she said with a smile.

Rachel Delahaye was born in Australia but has lived in the UK since she was six years old. She studied linguistics and worked as a magazine writer and editor before becoming a children's author. She loves words and animals; when she can combine the two, she is very happy indeed! At home, Rachel loves to read, write and watch wildlife documentaries. Outside, she loves to go walking in woodland. She also follows news about animal rights and the environment and hopes that one day the world will be a better home for all species, not just humans!

Rachel has two lively children and a dog called Rocket, and lives in the beautiful city of Bath.